TIMMY
and the Whales

by
Jeremy Moray

Illustrated by
Dee Gale

Published by Freedom 79 Publications Inc.
Vancouver, Canada

AUTHOR'S NOTE

I would like to thank Lens & Shutter, whose generosity helped towards the making of this book.

My thanks, again, to Gary Kleaman of Lionsgate Tug and Barge (1973) Ltd., for his patience in answering my many questions; and to those friends who have made this series of books possible.

J.M.

Canadian Cataloguing in Publication Data.

Moray, Jeremy, 1943-
   Timmy and the Whales

   ISBN 0-919131-01-8

   I. Gale, Dee.   II. Title.
   PS8576.073T45   jC813'.54   C80-091257-8
   PZ7.M673Tim

Published in Canada by
Freedom 79 Publications Inc., 302-2014 West Third Avenue, Vancouver, B.C., Canada, V6J 1L5.
Printed by D. W. Friesen & Sons Ltd., Cloverdale, B.C.
Typography: ITC Bookman by POLA/graphics Ltd.
Layout: Painter and Green Artists Ltd.

First Edition October 1980
Reprinted May 1981

Other Publications from Freedom 79:
   Timmy the West Coast Tug.
   The Merry Music-Makers Colouring Book.

for
Colin

ANOTHER AUTHOR'S NOTE

Don't forget to follow the story on the chart at
the back of this book.

J.M.

It was a very windy summer morning. Timmy the Tug was on his way to Crofton Mill on Vancouver Island. He was going to collect a barge full of heavy equipment and bring it back to a dockyard in False Creek in Vancouver. Here it would be stored until it was needed for another job. He had left his mooring on Granville Island very early. The journey would take all day.

The sea was rough. Timmy was having fun bouncing from wave to wave as he steamed across Georgia Strait. In the wheelhouse, Matilda, the tug's cat, was sitting in a corner. She was feeling a bit seasick, and hadn't even touched her bowl of milk.

Captain Jones turned to the mate Frank and said: "Timmy really likes this sort of weather."

"As long as it doesn't get much rougher," replied Frank, finishing his morning mug of tea. "We want to get that barge back before sunset."

Timmy smiled to himself as a large wave rolled him to one side. Spray splashed onto his foredeck.

"Simon's missing all the fun," he thought as he rolled back the other way.

Simon the seagull was Timmy's great friend. He went everywhere with him. However, he had decided that it was too rough to ride on Timmy today.

He had flown over, instead. He had said that he would wait for Timmy and the crew at Porlier Pass, on the other side of the strait.

Another wave lifted Timmy high in the air. He thought he saw a large black and white monster leap out of the water. It quickly disappeared again. Then there was another. And another.

When he got closer he could see they were killer whales. All of them were playing at jumping the waves as they swam northwards up the strait.

"Where are you going?" called Timmy.

"We're going to cheer on Wally and his swimming team. They have a swimming match up at Lasqueti Island."

Matilda could hear all the splashing, and the whistling noises that the whales were making. She staggered out onto the deck and waved to a baby whale.

Just then Timmy saw Wally surface a little way ahead of him. Wally the killer whale was one of Timmy's special friends.

"Good luck, Wally," Timmy called.

"Thanks; see you later." Wally squirted a fountain of water high into the air. Then he disappeared under the waves.

Soon, they could see the low lying islands of Galiano and Valdes. The narrow gap between them was Porlier Pass, one of the entrances to the Gulf Islands.

The two deckhands, John and Derek, were busy on deck. Suddenly, they heard cries of, "Help! Help!"

They looked up and saw a man and a woman on a small sailing boat, waving and shouting at them. The little boat was being blown onto the rocks, below the first lighthouse on Galiano Island.

John ran to the wheelhouse. He shouted to Captain Jones: "A boat is in trouble, Captain."

"Yes, I see it," replied Captain Jones. "Get a rope ready, John; we'll try to take it in tow."

Matilda didn't want to miss the excitement. She jumped up beside the wheel, and peered out of the window. She really felt much better.

"Don't you get in the way, Matilda," said Frank.
Matilda only blinked and twitched her tail.

Just then Simon flew over Timmy.

"Hello, Simon; we're going to rescue that sailboat," Timmy called excitedly.

"You'd better be quick. They're getting very close to the rocks. It won't be deep enough for you," Simon squawked.

Captain Jones stuck his head out of a window, and shouted to Simon: "Go and tell them we'll get as close as we can. Then we'll throw them a rope."

"O.K.," called Simon. He did a few twirls in the air, as he was caught by the strong wind.

Captain Jones brought Timmy closer to the sailboat. He had to be very careful. The wind and waves could easily bump Timmy against it. Frank went back to the aft deck to help John, and Matilda dashed out of the wheelhouse behind him. She climbed up onto the cabin roof for a better view.

The big waves were crashing on the rocks nearby.

Derek called from the foredeck: "It's getting very shallow, Captain. We're on the edge of the kelp." He could see the long strands of brown seaweed riding on the surface. He knew that wherever there was kelp, there would be rocks under the water.

As the little boat drifted helplessly, John threw the rope. The man tried to catch it, but the rope fell into the sea.

"We can't get any closer," Captain Jones called. As he turned Timmy in a circle, away from the boat, Simon dived down to the surface of the water. He picked up the end of the rope in his beak, and just managed to fly with it to the sailboat.

Matilda was jumping up and down so much with excitement that she nearly fell off the cabin roof.

"Good old Simon supergull!" she cried.

Timmy gently took up the strain on the rope, just before the sailboat hit the rocks. He pulled it very slowly into the middle of the pass.

"Suffering seaweed!" said Timmy. "Those people are lucky."

"Yes," agreed Captain Jones. "They were caught by the tide, and the current was too strong for their small engine. They should have checked their tide tables before setting out."

Timmy towed the sailboat into the harbour between the two lighthouses on Galiano Island. Once their little boat was safely tied up to the float, the people on board thanked Captain Jones very much for saving them. Then they threw a bun to Simon, and he caught it in the air.

"We'll remember the tides, next time," they called as Captain Jones took Timmy slowly out of the harbour.

When they had passed the second lighthouse, Frank took over the helm from Captain Jones. He set Timmy on a course to pass to the north of Hall Island. Then they passed the little island of Mowgli, south of Norway Island. Once they had steamed between Tent Island and the northern end of Saltspring, they reached the calmer waters of Stuart Channel.

Simon was very hungry after the rescue. He flew up in the air and called to Timmy that he was going to find some more food.

"You'll get so fat, you won't be able to fly!" said Matilda, lying in the sun on Timmy's foredeck.

Simon laughed as he glided away on the wind towards Saltspring Island.

It wasn't long before they were approaching Crofton Mill. Timmy gave a loud toot. He watched as two men walked down the wharf and stood waiting to take his mooring lines.

Once Timmy was tied up, Captain Jones went ashore to find out about the barge. John said he would cook some eggs for breakfast, so the rest of the crew followed him to the galley. Matilda had other ideas. She jumped onto the wharf and disappeared amongst the piles of lumber.

After breakfast, the crew went out on the aft deck to get the lines ready for towing the barge.

Meanwhile, Matilda had discovered some rats and mice. She was leaping and pouncing and racing after them, but they were too quick for her. They danced around teasing her, and waving their tails. Sometimes it seemed that they were chasing her, instead. They all knew she didn't really want to catch them. She just liked to play games.

Then Matilda saw a big fat mouse sitting near to Timmy. She crouched and got ready to pounce at it. She took a flying leap into the air. But she hadn't noticed Captain Jones coming back to the tug. She missed the mouse and landed right on Captain Jones' boot.

"Can't you tell I'm not a mouse, Matilda?" laughed Captain Jones, as he picked her off his boot. He put her on his shoulder, and climbed back on board Timmy.

Matilda felt very foolish. She went and sat on the stool in the wheelhouse, and pretended to read the charts.

Captain Jones called the crew together.

"They've changed our load," he said. "The machinery barge isn't ready to go, so we are going to take a barge loaded with four mobile homes."

Soon Timmy was moved gently up to the front of a large green and white barge. Derek and John fixed on the towline.

"Everything ready, then?" asked Captain Jones leaning out of the wheelhouse door.

"All ready to go, Captain," Frank said, as he walked along the side deck.

Captain Jones speeded up Timmy's engine, and moved him slowly away from the wharf.

"Ooh, good!" thought Timmy. "This is a nice light barge. It should be an easy trip."

So with his powerful engine roaring away, he was soon out into Stuart Channel again.

Matilda felt sleepy after her games at Crofton Mill. She went to have a cat-nap on the cabin roof.

They were passing the old Indian burial ground of Idol Island, when Frank noticed a large bald headed eagle circling above them. Matilda had seen it, too.

The eagle came lower and lower. Matilda was so frightened that she couldn't move. She put her paws over her head and meowed loudly, as a big dark shadow swept over her.

"Oh, no!" she cried. "He's going to grab me in his sharp claws, and have me for his lunch! Help me, someone!"

Again, the eagle circled. But this time he hovered over Matilda, ready to drop on his prey.

Frank saw what was happening. He tooted Timmy's horn loudly, to try to frighten the eagle away. But the eagle only swooped lower.

John came out of the galley. He heard Matilda crying for help. He ran to the ladder which was fixed to the side of the cabin. Climbing up onto the roof, he shouted at the eagle.

Suddenly, the sky was full of birds all squawking loudly, and diving at the eagle. Simon had quickly brought a crowd of seagulls and crows to the rescue.

"Don't worry, Matilda; we'll save you!" Simon called as he flew above her.

With an angry cry, the eagle finally flapped away followed by all the birds.

"Poor old Matilda," said John as he carried her down the ladder. "Let's get you a tin of your favourite salmon."

Matilda was so frightened she just clung onto John and shivered.

Once Simon had chased the eagle to its home on Idol Island, he flew back and settled on Timmy's bow.

"Well done, Simon," said Timmy. "That was very brave of you and your friends."

Just then Matilda came creeping round the corner of the wheelhouse.

"Are you all right, Matilda?" asked Simon.

"Yes; thanks to you, Simon," said Matilda. "But I think I've had enough adventure for one day."

As they all chatted about the eagle, Timmy steamed slowly back through Porlier Pass. The barge was now on a short towline, so that he could control it in the narrow waters.

Suddenly, Timmy rolled to one side as the first waves of Georgia Strait hit him. The wind was howling. The waves were bigger than they had been on the trip over that morning.

Frank called to John to tell him to get lunch ready.

"This is going to be a rough crossing," he said. "We'd better eat now, in case the weather gets worse."

When the first spray hit Timmy's deck, Matilda scurried into the wheelhouse. Simon settled down beside the funnel, out of the wind. Captain Jones came out of the cabin where he had been resting. He told Derek to let out a long towline. This would make Timmy's job easier in the rough sea. Then he went and joined Frank in the wheelhouse.

"It's going to be hard work for Timmy," he said as he closed one of the windows.

"Oh, he'll make it, all right," chuckled Frank. He held the wheel firmly as a big wave tried to turn Timmy.

Timmy wasn't nearly so happy now. He could feel the barge bumping around on the end of the towline. It also kept sliding from side to side. He had heard Captain Jones call this "fish-tailing". This made it harder work for Timmy, but he ploughed on bravely through the waves.

Big grey clouds were scudding across the sky. The rain began to pour down.

After several hours of very hard tugging, Timmy was beginning to feel tired. He was wondering if he would ever reach False Creek. Then, through the rain and spray, he saw the red bell buoy off Point Grey.

"Not long to go now," he thought. "We'll soon be home."

Suddenly, he lurched forwards, and banged into another wave.

"What's happened?" he cried. "I'm not pulling anything, anymore!"

Captain Jones and Frank were thrown forwards in the wheelhouse. Matilda clung onto the stool to stop herself from sliding across the floor.

"The towline's broken!" Captain Jones shouted. "I'll take the helm. Frank, you go back and help Derek."

Captain Jones slowed Timmy down.

Soon Frank returned.

"We'll have to try to get another line on the barge. Derek's getting it ready now," he said.

"Tell him to be quick," replied Captain Jones. "We must keep the barge off those sand banks."

They all knew it was a dangerous area. Because there was a very low tide, Timmy could see the sand stretching out a long way from the beach.

Timmy was very worried.

"I'll have to get awfully close to the barge for Derek to jump onto it with the line," he thought, nervously.

Captain Jones turned Timmy round and tried to steer him alongside the barge. Everytime they got near, a large wave would push them away. Again and again they tried, but it was no use.

All this time Matilda had been watching from the aft deck. As they turned to try again, she suddenly saw all the whales swimming past the entrance to English Bay.

She called excitedly to Simon: "That's Wally and his friends going home. Go and ask them to come and help us."

"Good idea," replied Simon. He flew off as fast as he could, calling to Wally as he went.

The barge drifted nearer and nearer to the sandbanks.

The wind was stronger now, and the rain was lashing down. The waves seemed huge to Timmy.

Captain Jones put Timmy's bows up against the side of the barge. He wanted to push it out into deeper water. Timmy's engine was going at full speed. He was pushing the barge as hard as he could.

"I can't go on much longer," he cried.

"Come on, Timmy," shouted Captain Jones. "You can do it! You've got to keep going until Wally gets here."

Just then, Wally appeared with his swimming team. He also had with him all the whale fans who had been to watch the match.

Soon he had them organised around the sides of the barge. He blew his whistle and they all pulled and pushed the barge out towards the bell buoy.

Once they were out of danger, Captain Jones called to Wally: "I'll take Timmy to the back of the barge and we'll push it. You get your whales along the two sides, and you can steer it for me."

"I'll help," said Simon. He flew up and sat on the front of the barge. If they had to go to the left, he would point with his left wing. If they had to go to the right, he would point with his right wing.

At last the rain stopped, and the wind died down. The summer storm was over, and the evening sun shone warmly.

It was getting late.

Captain Jones decided he would tie the barge up to the big red mooring buoy off Kitsilano beach for the night. They would tow it to the dock in the morning.

Slowly, they moved up English Bay into calmer water. By the time they got to the mooring buoy, there were crowds of people watching from the beach. Matilda went and stood on Timmy's bow and waved to them. Everyone else on board was busy tying up the barge.

Captain Jones thanked Wally and his whales for their help.

"Don't thank us; that was fun," replied Wally.

"I didn't think so," said a very tired Timmy.

"Never mind, Timmy; you made it safely. See you on your next trip." Wally gave him a pat with his flipper, as he swam smoothly past.

"I hope so, and thanks again," Timmy called.

Wally leapt high in the air, and then crashed down into the water.

"Well, let's get you home, Timmy. It's been a long day for you," said Captain Jones.

Timmy smiled to himself as he steamed slowly back into False Creek. Simon was so tired that he said goodnight and flew on ahead to his house under Granville bridge.

Soon, Timmy was alongside his mooring on Granville Island. By the time the crew had packed up their gear and climbed onto the wharf, he was fast asleep.

As Captain Jones walked home with Matilda, he saw a barge full of wood chips at the end of False Creek.

"Aha!" he said. "Maybe we'll be taking that one to the mill near Squamish on our next trip."

Matilda looked up and grinned.

THE END